The House Takes a Vacation

by Jacqueline Davies

illustrated by Lee White

MARSHALL CAVENDISH CHILDREN

When the Petersons left for vacation,
their house decided to go on holiday, too.

"Where shall we go?" asked the two bedroom windows.

The house had never been anywhere.

"We could visit the red house on the corner," said the window on the left.

"I'll lead the way!" shouted the front door.

"I'd rather visit the yellow house across the street," sniffed the window on the right.

"I'll lead the way!" shouted the front door.

"Dudes," said the roof, "there's no *way* I'm spending my vacation with the stuccoed-up houses in this neighborhood."

"I should like to see the sea," said the sunporch. "I've heard stories about the Dance of the Sunlight there."

"The sea," said the bedroom windows.

"The sea," said the roof.

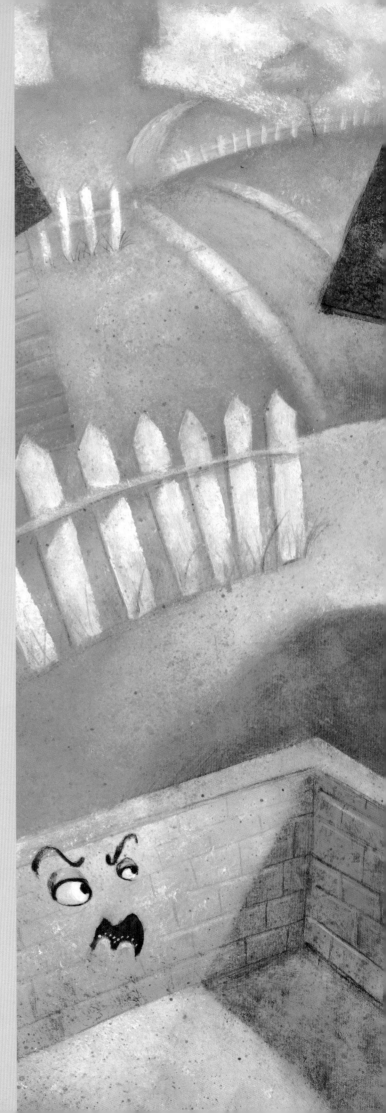

"I'll lead the way!" shouted the front door.

And so they all agreed. All except for the chimney, who didn't want to go anywhere. "Travel is a pain in the bricks," he complained in his smoky voice.

After examining a map, the house set off. The basement, however, stayed behind.

"You're such a stick-in-the-mud," said the roof, but the basement refused to rise to the occasion.

It took a whole day to make the trip.

Night had fallen by the time the house arrived. The beach was deserted and the sea was a silent blanket of blackness. The roof had fallen asleep.

"Wake up!" shouted the front door to the roof.

"Are we there yet?" mumbled the roof, stretching his gutters. "Man, am I sore. I feel like I've got shingles."

"I feel like I've got the flue," mumbled the chimney.

"Oh! The pane! The pane!" creaked the bedroom windows.

And then they all fell silent.
The house stared at the vast darkness.

"Is this it?" asked the bedroom windows.

"What a whole lot of zip wrapped up in nada," said the roof.

"I could have told you," said the chimney. "Travel never lives up to your expectations. It's better just to stay home."

"Let's go home!" said the bedroom windows.

"I'll lead the way!" shouted the front door.

"No," said the sunporch. "Let's stay the night. I want to see the Dance of the Sunlight. Then we will go home."

The house shifted uncomfortably.

"We could use the rest," said the windows. "We're nearly shattered from all this travel."

So the house settled down for the night, but no one got much sleep. The houseflies met up with the sand fleas and they had a party in the walls that didn't break up until dawn.

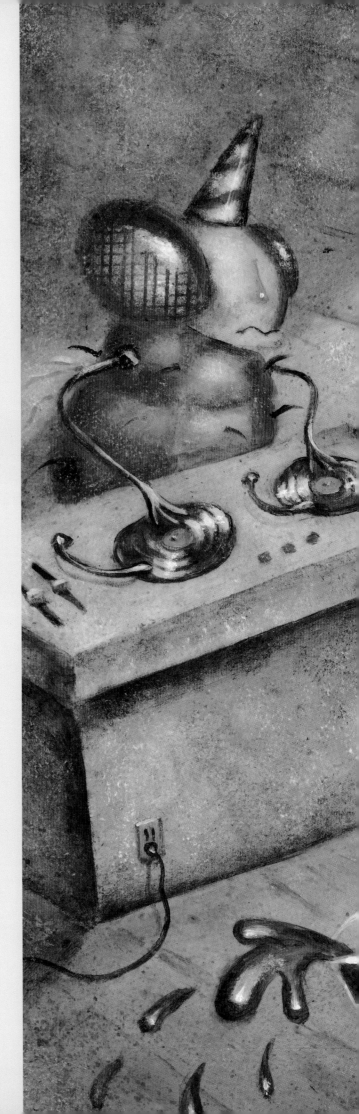

"Look," whispered the sunporch, who had stayed awake all night.

The front door creaked open. The chimney straightened up. The roof stretched and peaked. The bedroom windows shuddered their shutters. Everyone looked at the sea.

"That is something!" shouted the front door.

"Can't top that," said the roof.

"Lovely!" twittered the windows.

Even the chimney said, "Holy smoke."

The sunporch smiled as she felt the sun-warmed air flow through her screens. "I'm so glad we came," she said.

"Dudes!" said the roof. "Surf's up!"

"I'll lead the way!" shouted the front door.

"Do we dare?" squealed the bedroom windows.

"Why not?" roared the chimney. "You only live once!"

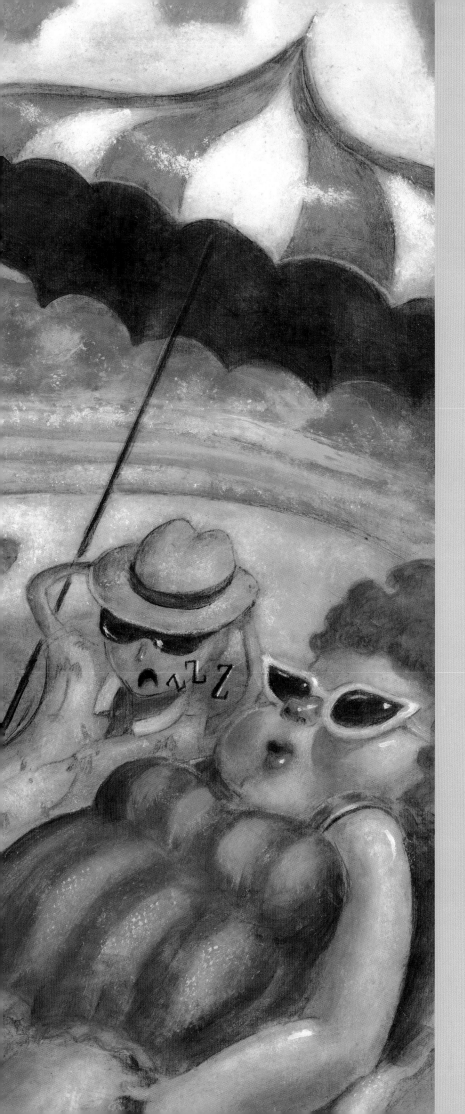

Without a moment's hesitation, the house went to the water's edge and dipped its foundation in. But it waded in too far, too fast, and was swept out to sea. Unable to stop, unable to steer, it drifted in the current.

The house sailed along for several miles before
it came to a lighthouse.

"Amateur," muttered the lighthouse as it pointed
the house toward the shore.

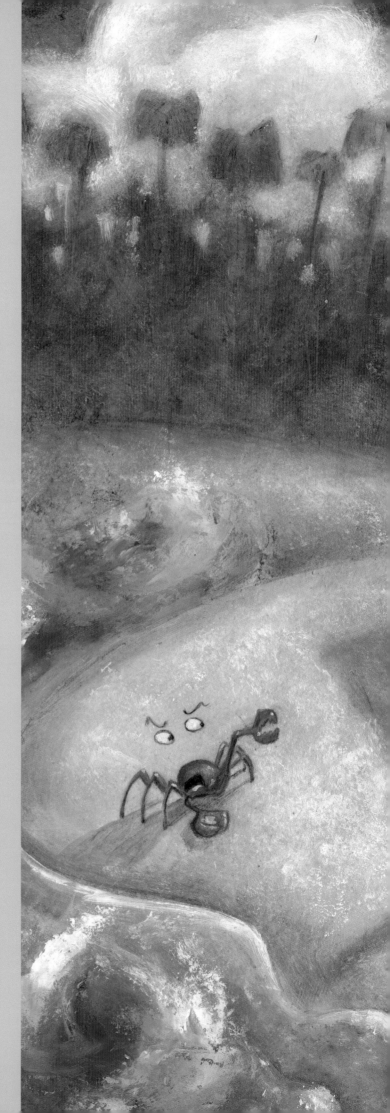

The house dragged itself out of the surf, shook the saltwater from its gutters, and began to hobble home.

"Never again," groaned the chimney, dropping bricks along the way.

The house made it home before it got dark. The basement, cracked and sunburned, was glad to be covered once more. Tired from their travel, everyone settled down quickly and fell asleep.

All through the night, the sunporch dreamed of the glorious Dance of the Sunlight and heard the whistling of the sea breeze. She was already planning their next vacation.

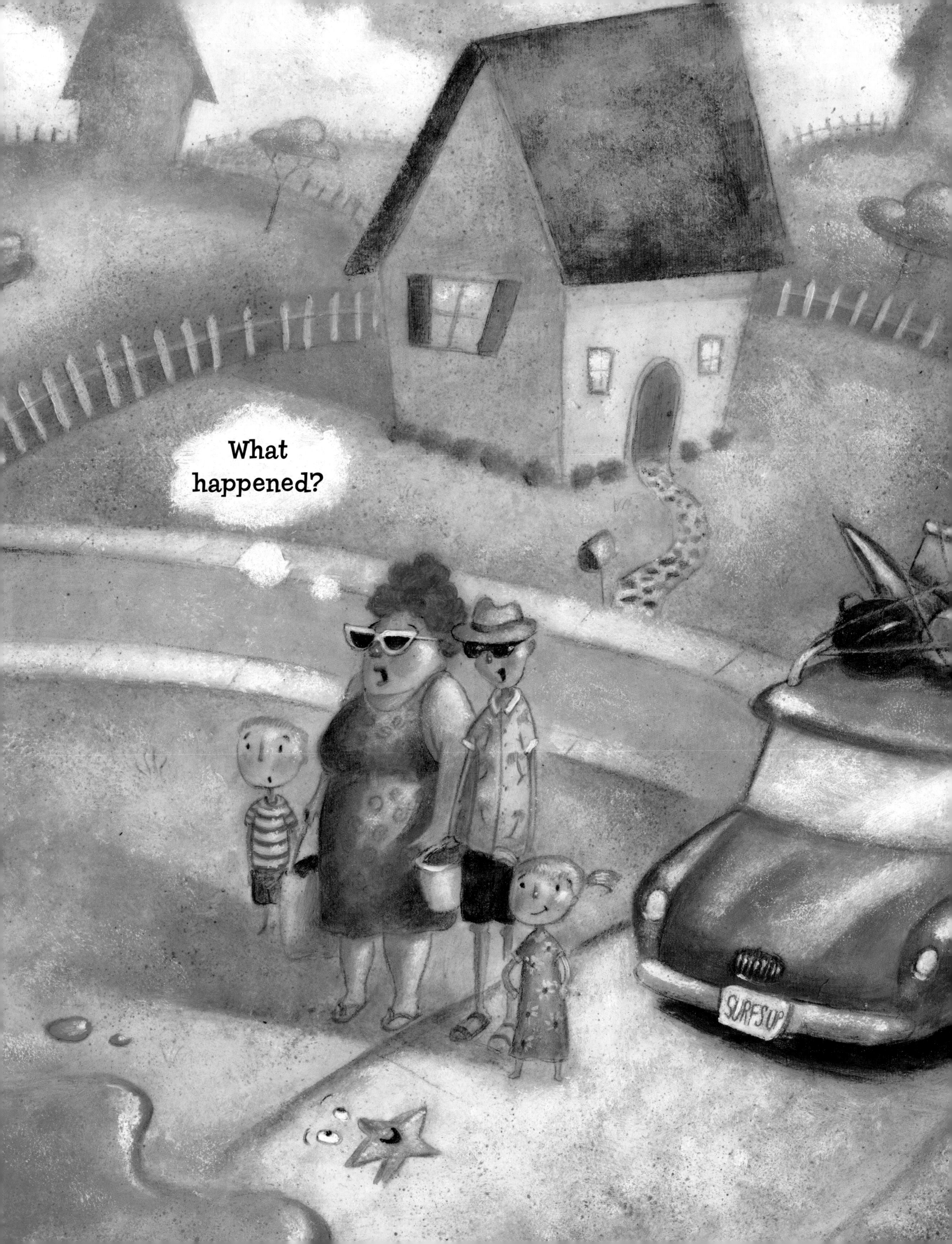
What happened?
SURFSUP

To Andrea Wong
— J.D.

To my dad Jim
— L.W.

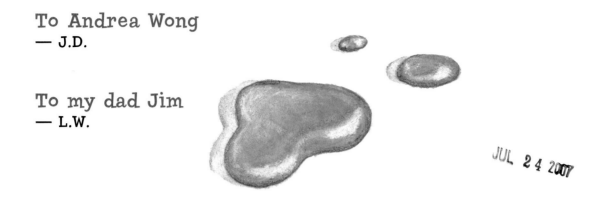

Text copyright © 2007 by Jacqueline Davies
Illustrations copyright © 2007 by Lee White

Marshall Cavendish Corporation, 99 White Plains Road, Tarrytown, NY 10591
www.marshallcavendish.us

Library of Congress Cataloging-in-Publication Data
Davies, Jacqueline, 1962-
The house takes a vacation / by Jacqueline Davies ; illustrations by Lee White.
p. cm.
Summary: While the Petersons are away, their house decides to take a trip
to the sea to watch the "Dance of the Sunlight," despite some groaning
from the chimney and the basement's refusal to rise to the occasion.
ISBN-13: 978-0-7614-5331-4
[1. Dwellings—Fiction. 2. Vacations—Fiction. 3. Seashore—Fiction. 4.
Humorous stories.] I. White, Lee, 1970- ill. II. Title.
PZ7.D29392Hou 2006
[E]—dc22
2006012991

The text of this set book is set in Chowderhead.
The illustrations are rendered in oil and colored pencil on illustration board.
Book design by Becky Terhune

Printed in China
First edition
1 3 5 6 4 2

mc Marshall Cavendish
Children